D0345304

WHY THIS IS AN EASY READER

- This story has been carefully written so that it will keep the young reader's interest high.
- It is told in a simple, open style with a strong rhythm that adds enjoyment both to reading aloud and silent reading.
- Only 102 different words have been used, with plurals, root words and compounds counted once.
- There is a very high percentage of words repeated. *It is this skillful repetition which helps the child to read independently.* Seeing words again and again, he "practices" the vocabulary he knows, and actually learns the words that are new.

ABOUT THE WORDS IN THIS STORY

- 80 words—*more than three-quarters of the total vocabulary*—have been used at least three times.
- Nearly two-thirds of the words have been used at least five times.
- One-fifth of the words have been used at least 22 times.
- Some words have been used 51 times.
- This story is marked by a strong, appealing rhythm that lends itself to oral reading and dramatization.

The Secret Cat

Story *by* TAMARA KITT

Pictures by WILLIAM RUSSELL

Editorial Consultant: LILIAN MOORE

WONDER BOOKS
A Division of Grosset & Dunlap, Inc.
New York, N.Y. 10010

Introduction

These books are meant to help the young reader discover what a delightful experience reading can be. The stories are such fun that they urge the child to try his new reading skills. They are so easy to read that they will encourage and strengthen him as a reader.

The adult will notice that the sentences aren't too long, the words aren't too hard, and the skillful repetition is like a helping hand. What the child will feel is: "This is a good story—and I can read it myself!"

For some children, the best way to meet these stories may be to hear them read aloud at first. Others, who are better prepared to read on their own, may need a little help in the beginning—help that is best given freely. Youngsters who have more experience in reading alone—whether in first or second or third grade—will have the immediate joy of reading "all by myself."

These books have been planned to help all young readers grow—in their pleasure in books and in their power to read them.

Lilian Moore
Specialist in Reading
Formerly of Division of Instructional Research,
New York City Board of Education

There was a prince

and there was

a princess.

7

There was a king

and there was

a queen.

The king was the father, of course.

The queen was the mother, of course.

And, of course,

the prince was the little boy.

And, of course,

the princess was the little girl.

And oh, yes! There was . . .

. . . a cat.

He was a secret cat.

The king did not know
about the cat.
The queen did not know
about the cat.

He was the secret cat
of the prince and princess.
And they loved him.

The cat was very smart.

You will see how smart he was.

You will see how he helped
the prince and princess.

The prince and the princess are sad.

Today is the queen's birthday.

And they do not have
a birthday present to give her.

"It is a shame," the princess says.
"It is a dirty shame.
I am a princess,
and you are a prince,
and we cannot get
a birthday present
to give Mom, the queen."

"We can sell our crowns,"
says the prince.

"Sell our crowns?" the princess says.

"NO!

You are a prince.

A prince cannot sell his crown.

I am a princess.

A princess cannot sell her crown."

"What can we do?" says the prince.

"Meow!"

The cat is trying to say,

"I know what you can do."

20

"I know what we can do,"
says the prince.
"That is a smart cat.
Maybe we can trade him
for something.
Then we will have a present
for Mom, the queen."

"Trade our cat?" the princess says.

"Meow!"

The cat is trying to say,

"Why not?"

"Oh, well, why not?"

the princess says.

She puts a big bow on the cat.

She kisses him.

And she says, "Let's go."

So they go—

the prince,

the princess,

and the cat.

They see a man

on a big white horse.

"Hello," says the man.

"Hello," says the prince.

"That is a fine horse you have."

"That is a fine cat you have,"
says the man.

"He is a smart cat, too,"
the princess says.

The cat does a trick.

"He IS a smart cat," the man says.

"He is a very smart cat.

Will you trade?

Give me the cat,

and I will give you my horse."

"A horse is a fine present

for Mom, the queen,"

says the prince.

"No," the princess says.
"The man likes our cat
better than the horse.
Maybe our cat
IS better than the horse."

"Meow!"

The cat is trying to say,

"That's right."

"Yes. That's right," says the prince.

"We will not trade our cat

for your horse.

Thank you. Good-by."

Now they see a man

with a big blue bag.

"Hello," says the man.

"Hello," says the prince.

"That is a fine bag

you have."

"That is a fine cat you have,"
says the man.
"He is a smart cat, too,"
the princess says.

The cat does a trick.

"He IS a smart cat," the man says.

"He is a very smart cat.

Will you trade?

Give me the cat,

and I will give you my big bag

with all these things."

"A big bag is a fine present
for Mom, the queen,"
says the prince.

"No," the princess says.
"The man likes our cat
better than the big bag.
Maybe our cat IS better
than the big bag
with all those things."

"Meow!" the cat says.

The cat is trying to say,
"That's right."

"Yes. That's right," says the prince.
"We will not trade our cat
for your bag.
Thank you. Good-by."

Now they see a lady
with a ring made of gold.
"Hello," says the lady.
"Hello," says the prince.
"That is a fine ring
you have."

"That is a fine cat you have,"
says the lady.
"He is a smart cat, too,"
the princess says.

The cat does a trick.

"He IS a smart cat," the lady says.
"Will you trade?
Give me your cat,
and I will give you my ring
made of gold."

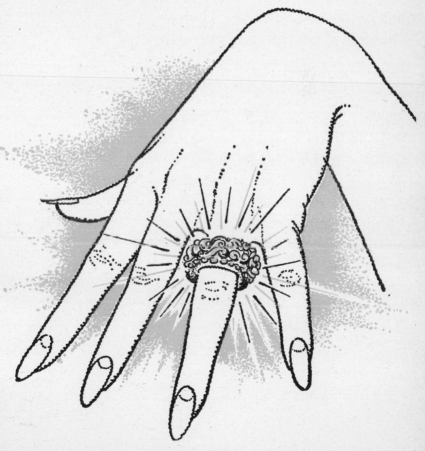

"A ring is a fine present for Mom, the queen," says the prince.

"No," the princess says.

"The lady likes our cat
better than the ring.

Maybe our cat IS better
than the ring made of gold."

"Meow!" the cat says.

The cat is trying to say,

"That's right."

"Yes. That's right," says the prince.
"We will not trade our cat
for your ring.
Thank you. Good-by."

Now it is time to go home.
"We still do not have
a birthday present
for Mom, the queen,"
says the prince.

"Yes, we do! Yes, we do!"

the princess says.

"We have a fine present.

It is better

than a ring made of gold.

It is better

than a big blue bag.

It is better

than a big white horse.

You will see."

"Meow!" the cat says.

The cat is trying to say,

"THAT'S RIGHT."

Now it is time

for the birthday present.

"Happy birthday!" says the prince.

The princess says,

"Happy birthday,

dear Mom, the queen.

Happy birthday to you!"

"Thank you!"

The queen is very happy.

The king says,

"A cat is a fine present."

The prince and princess are happy.

The queen has a birthday present.

But they are sad, too.

Now they do not have a secret cat.

Now they do not have a cat at all.

They say good-by to the cat

and they go out.

"Meow! Meow!"

The cat is trying to say,

"Wait! Wait! I am coming, too.

I am the queen's birthday present,
but I am *your* cat!"